MR.
BEAST

For Charlie — J. S.

For Greta, Emilio, and Loveday,
from Grumpy Trousers — R. A.

Henry Holt and Company, LLC
Publishers since 1866
115 West 18th Street
New York, New York 10011
www.henryholt.com

Henry Holt is a registered trademark of Henry Holt and Company, LLC
Text copyright © 2004 by James Sage
Illustrations copyright © 2004 by Russell Ayto
All rights reserved.
First published in the United States in 2005 by Henry Holt and Company
Originally published in the United Kingdom in 2004 by HarperCollins Publishers Ltd.
Distributed in Canada by H. B. Fenn and Company Ltd.

Library of Congress Cataloging-in-Publication Data
Sage, James.
Mr. Beast / James Sage; illustrated by Russell Ayto.—1st American ed.
p.   cm.
Summary: When Charlie eats up all of his mother's homemade doughnuts, his neighbor Mr. Beast threatens to eat Charlie up.
ISBN-13: 978-0-8050-7730-8
ISBN-10: 0-8050-7730-8
[1. Monsters—Fiction.] I. Title: Mister Beast. II. Ayto, Russell, ill. III. Title.
PZ7.S1304Mr 2005   [E]—dc22   2004024281

First American Edition—2005
Printed in Singapore

1 3 5 7 9 10 8 6 4 2

MR. BEAST

James Sage

illustrated by Russell Ayto

Henry Holt and Company

New York

Charlie loved sugared doughnuts almost as much as he loved monsters.

Which is why his mom said to him one day, "Charlie, my pet, if I had a larger frying pan, I'd make some of your favorite sugared doughnuts. Go and ask Mr. Beast if I can borrow his big old black one."

So Charlie set off down the path.

"With pleasure!" gushed Mr. Beast, picking his ugly, sharp teeth with a **twing** and a **twang**. "But tell your dear mother that I expect to have my big old black pan returned filled to the brim with her delectable doughnuts!"

So Charlie lugged the frying pan home, and his mom made him as many doughnuts as he could eat. (Which was a lot!)

Then she made a batch for Mr. Beast, which Charlie lugged back.

But on the way, Charlie began to eat those doughnuts, too. . . .

...And he kept on eating them ...

...until there was only one pathetic little doughnut left.

And then he ate
THAT!

"It's my sweet tooth," explained Charlie.

But such a lame excuse did not satisfy Mr. Beast. "You've eaten all my doughnuts, bozo, so tonight I'll eat you! Depend upon it!"

And he slammed the door.

When Charlie told his mom that Mr. Beast was planning to eat him, she said she was very sorry indeed to hear that as she would miss him terribly, but she would try not to fret.

Then Charlie went through the house . . .

. . . and checking to see that Mr. Beast . . .

...locking all the doors ...   ...and shutting all the windows ...

...wasn't already lurking in the broom closet or hiding behind the fish tank.

Not long afterward Charlie
went to bed—but not to sleep!
For it was then that Mr. Beast
came visiting, just as he said
he would!

"I'm going to eat you up, Charlie boy," he called. "I'm outside now!"

Shuffle

Rumble

Grunt!

And Charlie could hear
Mr. Beast clambering up
the creeper!

Crickle

Crackle

Crunch!

And then Charlie could hear
Mr. Beast clattering about
on the roof!

Piddle

Paddle

Plunk!

"I'm coming to eat
you up. Yes, I am!"

And then Charlie could hear
Mr. Beast stuffing himself into
the chimney!

Squiggle
Shimmy...

And then sliding down it!

...swish
Slither...
Slump!

"Now I'm in the house, and I'm really going to eat you up!" he shouted.

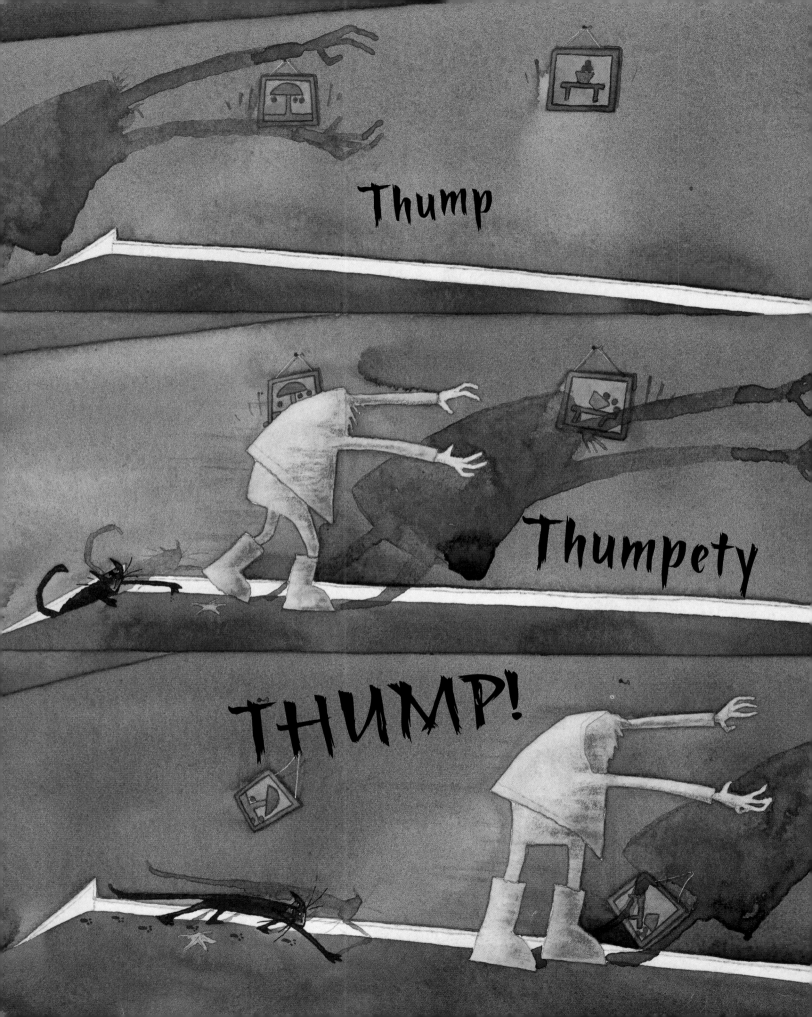

And Charlie could hear Mr. Beast stomping along the hall!

Then Charlie heard Mr. Beast
kick open the bedroom door
with one mighty thrust of
his great big foot …

...and walk right in!

Blim

Blam

BLUMP!

And when Charlie heard this he did what any brave person would do under the circumstances. He made himself as little as possible.

YEEHAW!

howled Mr. Beast as he yanked back the bedcovers. "And now I really and truly will EAT YOU UP!"

And he tickled Charlie all over while roaring in a very beastly voice, "YUM! YUMMY! YUM!" as Charlie shouted, "BUT IT'S ONLY ME, DADDY, IT'S ONLY ME!"

Such a racket naturally brought Charlie's mom hurrying upstairs.

She told Mr. Beast to act his age if he possibly could, as it was already way past Charlie's bedtime....

She told Charlie to say good night and go to sleep without delay!

Charlie and Mr. Beast promised to be as good as gold from that moment on . . .

. . . and the funny thing was,

they really meant it!